S0-BZT-960

# EVEN SUPERHEROES MAKE MISTAKES

# MAGNIFIQUE

# SCREECHER

TYPHOON

ICKY

**To Reena. Thanks for the SUPER idea,
and for all your encouragement and support! —S. B.**

**For the super Salibas —E. K.**

No part of this publication may be reproduced, stored in a retrieval system, or transmitted in any form or by any means, electronic, mechanical, photocopying, recording, or otherwise, without written permission of the publisher. For information regarding permission, write to Sterling Publishing Co., Inc., 1166 Avenue of the Americas, New York, NY 10036.

ISBN 978-1-338-53246-3

Interior text copyright © 2018 by Shelly Becker. Cover and interior illustrations copyright © 2018 by Eda Kaban. All rights reserved. Published by Scholastic Inc., 557 Broadway, New York, NY 10012, by arrangement with Sterling Publishing Co., Inc. SCHOLASTIC and associated logos are trademarks and/or registered trademarks of Scholastic Inc.

The publisher does not have any control over and does not assume any responsibility for author or third-party websites or their content.

12 11 10 9 8 7 6 5 4 3 2          19 20 21 22 23 24

Printed in the U.S.A.          40

First Scholastic printing, January 2019

The artwork for this book was created digitally.

# EVEN SUPERHEROES MAKE MISTAKES

By SHELLY BECKER · Illustrated by EDA KABAN

SCHOLASTIC INC.

When superheroes are not up to speed,
when they slip up, and trip up, and fail to succeed . . .

. . . they could cry, or deny, or claim it's not fair

or rip off their capes and quit in despair.

If they bake super-cakes with way too much salt,
they could shrug, "It was bakery bought—not *my* fault!"

If they bungle their speech at the Hero Convention,
they could put on a light show, diverting attention.

If they space out and nab the wrong guys without thought,
they could choose to let bandits succeed with their plot!

**B**ut ashamed superheroes who goofed up somehow . . .

first **STOP** and consider what's best to do **NOW**.

If they wake late for boot camp the very first day,
they invent an alarm clock that works right away.

If last year they ruined the annual choir,
they train screechy voices and learn to sing higher.

If they didn't prepare any clean clothes to wear,

they still polish
their boots

and spiff up their hair.

But if superheroes can't take their errors in stride,
they might look for a way to excuse, blame, or hide.

If they bash through the planets while flying in space,

they could claim someone's cape was obstructing their face.

If they build a big bridge that doesn't sit right,
they could blame and call names—
a super-charged fight!

If their rescue attempt was **NOT** super-clever,
they could stock up supplies and hide out FOREVER.

When superheroes are not up to speed,
when they slip up, and trip up, and fail to succeed . . .

they *could* hang their heads down, they *could*, but they *don't!*
Because *real* superheroes just *wouldn't*, they *won't!*

Instead they remember perfection is rare,
And they choose super ways to respond when they err.

And using their powers as true heroes do . . .
they fix what they wrecked and apologize, too!

They fess up their mess-up. They learn from their blooper.
RESPONSIBILITY! THAT makes them SUPER!

It's okay if they blush.

It's okay if they quake.

It's okay if they super-regret their mistake!

But then they get up and get on with their day . . .

. . . saving the world in their most super way.

BEASTIE          ZING

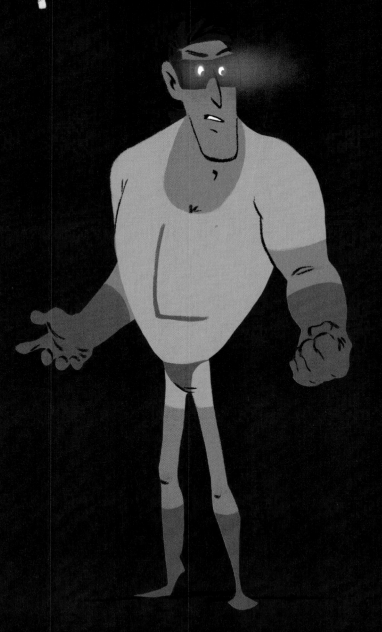

**THRASH** **LASERMAN**

**SHELLY BECKER** is the author of several books for young readers, including *Mine! Mine! Mine!*, which has been included in many top 5 and top 10 lists of books to teach the concept of sharing. Although Shelly does not have a cape or laser vision, she knows how it feels to make mistakes and tries to use her inner superpowers to respond in a positive way. She hopes her books will encourage readers of all ages to do the same. She lives in Toronto, Canada.

**EDA KABAN** was born and raised in Turkey and studied illustration in the United States. She has illustrated several children's books and her illustrations have been recognized by the Society of Illustrators, *Creative Quarterly*, American Illustration, and *3X3*. When she is not drawing or dreaming of fighting crime, she climbs rocks and bikes the hills of the Bay Area. She lives in Oakland, California, with her husband.